ME and MR. MAH

ME and MR. MAH

written by **Andrea Spalding**

illustrated by **Janet Wilson**

ORCA BOOK PUBLISHERS

I met Mr. Mah the summer we moved. Mom and Dad had split.

Dad stayed on the farm and Mom took me to the city, a thousand miles away.

We might as well have gone to the moon. The yard was a moonscape — patchy grass and dirt, surrounded by a prison-like fence.

I squinted through a gap in the fence. Next door, a man in a Chinese hat was working in a vegetable garden. There were no kids.

Everyone had a job except me.

I tried to help the movers. "Beat it, kid," the big one growled.

"Ian, why don't you stay in the yard while we bring in the furniture?" Mom tornadoed around the house, organizing.

I made myself as small as I felt ... and waited ... and waited ... for my special shoe box.

"I'll take that." I grabbed the box, ran into the backyard and eagerly lifted the lid.

The familiar smell of hay tickled my nose. Tucked in the middle were the sun-bleached cow bones Dad and I had found on the prairie walk and the tiny tractor he'd given me — just like his.

"I miss you, Dad," I whispered.

I ran the tractor along the base of the fence, then peered through the crack again. The man was still working in his garden.

A mover dumped another box by the back door. "Hey kid," he shouted, "this says 'gardening equipment.' Is it okay out here?"

"Guess so," I shrugged.

I ripped the box open. Out tumbled a trowel and small fork, the watering can and leather gloves. Grabbing the trowel, I headed back to the soft earth by the fence to make a field for my tractor. The earth smelled dark and chocolaty like Dad's farm.

All week I ploughed, until I'd turned a strip along one length of the fence.

The man next door worked all week, too. Each time I peeked, he was digging or weeding. His plot was full of growing things.

One morning I found a packet of sunflower seeds tucked through the gap in the fence. I wedged a chocolate chip cookie through the crack, then I planted the seeds like the man next door.

The next day I heard a hissing sound and peered through. He'd hooked up his hose and was watering his plants.

I watered my seeds.

I looked through the fence to see what he'd do next.

Yikes ... a dark eye looked back. "You like to visit Mr. Mah's garden?" said a voice.

Mr. Mah's garden was a knee-high jungle.

"Gai Lan and Bok Choy — Chinese broccoli and cabbages," he explained, "... and sunflowers."

We both laughed.

Mr. Mah let me touch and nibble and smell my way up and down the rows of unfamiliar vegetables until my back ached.

"You like tea?"

Mr. Mah's teapot had a gold dragon wiggling around the side. So did the cups — small cups, like egg cups.

"Is this a doll's tea set?" I asked.

Mr. Mah laughed and shook his head. "Chinese cups are small. Not for dolls ... for everyone."

Mr. Mah told stories of China. Of farming rice in paddies, and going to work on bicycles. I told stories of wheat farming on the prairies, and riding the combine harvester.

Mr. Mah showed me how he frightened crows away from his plants.

I tied tinfoil strips over my sunflower seedlings.

Mr. Mah said my name in a special way. "Yan," he called through the fence after our gardening. "Yan, you like to visit?"

Yan means wild goose in Chinese.

I wish Mom and I were wild geese. Then we could fly back to Dad's farm and be a family again.

Mr. Mah's family visited every weekend. I watched them through the fence.

No one visited us. Mr. Mah was my best friend.

Once Mr. Mah and I went for a walk through the Chinese cemetery. He told me there used to be a bone house, where the long-dead Chinese waited for their families to raise the money to send their bones back to China.

"Do they do that now?" I asked.

Mr. Mah shook his head. "No. We are Canadian. We stay here."

I built a bone house out of moving boxes. I sat inside and decided I'd stay until Mom took us back to the prairies ... but it rained, and my bone house was ruined.

Mr. Mah took me to Chinatown. We looked at the Chinese gate and rubbed the lion's tongue for good luck. I bought a dragon rice bowl and Mr. Mah gave me some chopsticks. I used them every morning to eat my cereal.

One afternoon I showed Mr. Mah my special box. He smelled the hay and admired the cow bones. As he looked at the tractor, I told him about my dad.

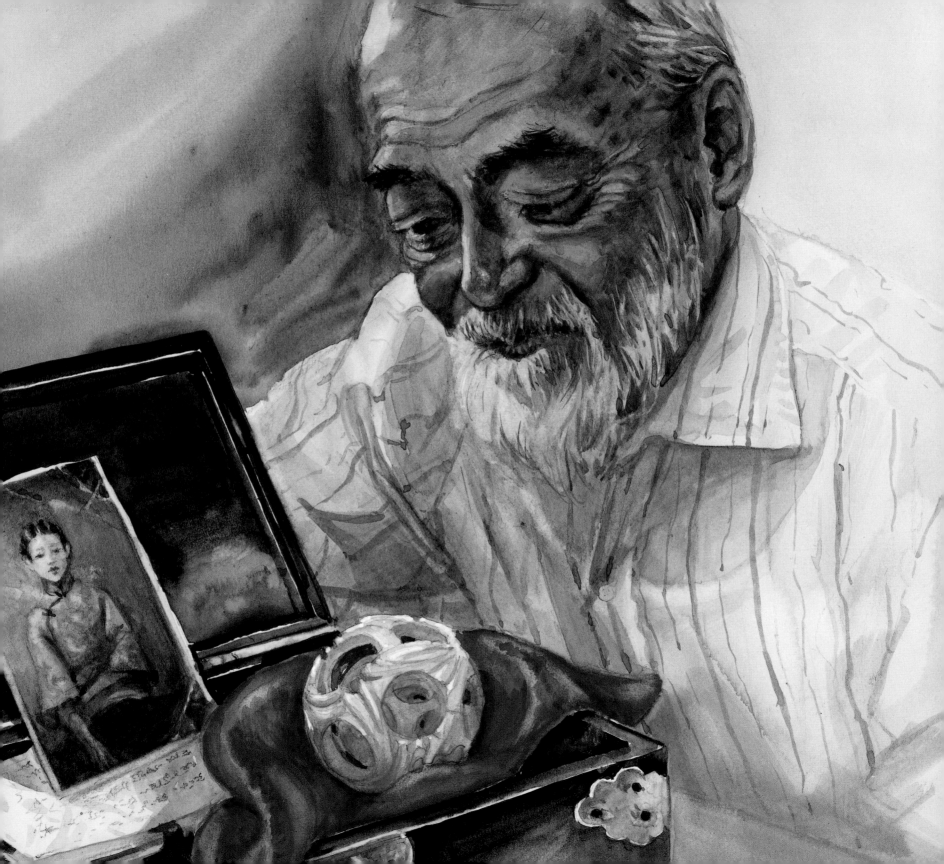

The next day Mr. Mah showed me his special box.

I didn't know grownups had special boxes. Mr. Mah's was really special. It was black lacquer and fastened with a gold clasp.

Mr. Mah unfastened the clasp and lifted the lid. We could smell China — sandalwood, incense and herbs. Inside were mystery things wrapped in red silk, a letter in Chinese, a small carved ball with an even smaller ball inside, and a photograph.

"My wife," said Mr. Mah.

"Where's your wife now?" I blurted out.

Mr. Mah looked sad. "Very sick last year. She died."

"Here," I said, "you can have my tractor."

Mr. Mah smiled, but shook his head. "Chinese boxes keep Chinese memories." He gently shut the lid and refastened the clasp.

I painted my special box shiny black. When it was dry I replaced the hay, the tractor, the chopsticks and bones. On top I laid my postcards from Dad. My special box was filling up.

When my sunflowers reached full height, summer was almost over. Mom said the divorce settlement was through and she'd bought a tiny house near my new school.

"With a yard that's not a moonscape?" I asked.

She nodded.

"I'll take some sunflower seeds anyway," I said.

Me and Mr. Mah hugged. He gave me his ball-within-a-ball for good luck and I promised to visit.

Our house was on the other side of the city, and it wasn't a moonscape. I could glimpse the ocean from the climbing rock in the front yard and swing from a rope on the oak tree in the back. There were kids on our street, and I made friends with Randy. He taught me to rollerblade, and we joined a soccer club.

One evening Mom took me into a secondhand store to look for furniture. "If you find a small desk for your room, we'll buy it," she said.

I pushed aside some chairs and poked around. On a dusty shelf I saw a black lacquer box with a gold clasp, just like Mr. Mah's. I opened the clasp and lifted the lid. It smelled like China.

"Mom," I yelled. "Something terrible's happened to Mr. Mah. Here's his special box."

"There are lots of boxes like this," said Mom. "There's no reason to believe it's Mr. Mah's."

But I knew it was. For caught in the hinge was a scrap of red silk, just like the piece that wrapped his memories.

We brought the box home, and that night I phoned Mr. Mah.

"This number is no longer in service," said a voice on the telephone.

I found the phone book and phoned every Mah listed until I found someone who knew my Mr. Mah.

"Mr. Mah fell and broke his hip," explained his daughter-in-law. "He's bedridden in a home and would love to see you."

Mom drove me to the home.

I took the black lacquer box and gave it back to Mr. Mah.

"My daughter-in-law sold it by mistake," he said.

We laughed, but our eyes watered.

I closed his fingers over the carved ball-within-a-ball. "So your Chinese box has a Chinese memory again," I said.

Mr. Mah returned the ball, but placed my "Get Well" picture inside his box.

"My Chinese box has the memory of Yan."

Mr. Mah and I are still best friends. He tells me about China and his family.

I talk about my dad and describe my new home and new friends. Sometimes I bring Mr. Mah interesting things I've made. His special box is filling up.

And I've just planted his sunflower seeds again.

For Charles, with love.
A.S.

With great affection to
W. Harold McCamus R.C.A.F.
J.W.

Text copyright © 1999 Brandywine Enterprises
Illustration copyright © 1999 Janet Wilson

Canadian Cataloguing in Publication Data
Spalding, Andrea.
Me and Mr. Mah

ISBN 1-55143-168-8

I. Wilson, Janet, 1952– II. Title.
PS8587.P213M4 1999   jC813'.54   C99-910539-6
PZ7.S7335Me 1999

Library of Congress Catalog Card Number: 99-63059

Orca Book Publishers gratefully acknowledges the support of our publishing programs provided by the following agencies: The Government of Canada through the Book Publishing Industry Development Program (BPIDP), The Canada Council for the Arts, and the British Columbia Arts Council.

Design by Christine Toller

Printed and bound in Hong Kong

Orca Book Publishers
PO Box 5626, Station B
Victoria, BC Canada
V8R 6S4

Orca Book Publishers
PO Box 468
Custer, WA USA
98240-0468

01 00 99 5 4 3 2 1

Canadä